W9-BRI-850

Larchmont Public Library
Larchmont New York 10538

IN THE
HEART
OF THE
VILLAGE

TREE 𐆖 TALES

IN THE HEART OF THE VILLAGE

The World of the Indian Banyan Tree

BARBARA BASH

Sierra Club Books for Children · San Francisco

The Sierra Club, founded in 1892 by John Muir, has devoted itself to the study and protection of the earth's scenic and ecological resources — mountains, wetlands, woodlands, wild shores and rivers, deserts and plains. The publishing program of the Sierra Club offers books to the public as a nonprofit educational service in the hope that they may enlarge the public's understanding of the Club's basic concerns. The point of view expressed in each book, however, does not necessarily represent that of the Club. The Sierra Club has some sixty chapters in the United States and in Canada. For information about how you may participate in its programs to preserve wilderness and the quality of life, please address inquiries to Sierra Club, 85 Second Street, San Francisco, CA 94105.

Copyright © 1996 by Barbara Bash

All rights reserved under International and Pan-American Copyright Conventions. No part of this book may be reproduced in any form or by any electronic or mechanical means, including information storage and retrieval systems, without permission in writing from the publisher.

First Edition

All calligraphy by Barbara Bash

The author wishes to express her appreciation to Jon Beckmann for his clear vision in recognizing potential and supporting its growth.

Author's note: The Nirantali creation story that opens this book was adapted from a folktale from the Indian state of Orissa. The principal sources for this retelling were *A Study of Orissan Folklore* by K. B. Das (Visvabhariti University Santiniketan, 1953) and *Tribal Myths of Orissa* by Verrier Elwin (Oxford University Press, 1954).

Library of Congress Cataloging-in-Publication Data
Bash, Barbara.
    In the heart of the village: the world of the Indian Banyan tree/Barbara Bash.
        p. cm. — (Tree tales)
    Summary: Describes the importance of a banyan tree to an Indian village.
    ISBN 0-87156-575-7 (alk. paper)
    1. Banyan tree — India — Juvenile literature. 2. Banyan tree — Ecology — India — Juvenile literature. 3. Banyan tree — India — Folklore — Juvenile literature. 4. Folklore — India — Juvenile literature. [1. Banyan tree — India.] I. Title. II. Series: Bash, Barbara. Tree tales.
QK495.M73B27 1996
583'.962 — dc20   95-51345

Printed in Hong Kong

10 9 8 7 6 5 4 3 2 1

To my husband
Steve
who led me to
India

5/97 B+T

In the ancient times, Nirantali, the first mother of the earth, was sent by the gods to create the world. She carried with her tiny banyan seeds wrapped in leaves.

First she made the sun, the moon, and the earth; then she created human beings. But the sun beat down on the people, and they felt hot all the time because they had no shade. So Nirantali gave them the banyan seeds to plant.

The seeds grew into small trees with tiny leaves that provided no shade at all. So Nirantali took the leaves and began to pull. She tugged and tugged until the leaves were large. Then she stretched the banyan branches until they reached all the way down to the ground.

Soon people came from all around to sit together in the shade of the tree. This is how the banyan came to grow in the heart of the village.

Like a great green mountain, the banyan tree rests on the earth. From its center, broad branches extend outward, sprouting aerial roots that hang down like snakes. When they grow long enough to reach the ground, they take root and thicken, becoming wooden pillars. Supported by these trunks, the branches spread out further and further. In this way, a single tree can become a forest, covering many acres.

The banyan tree grows in many tropical areas of the world— India, Indonesia, Hawaii, Florida, the

Caribbean. Its leaves are green throughout the seasons, and several times a year ruby red figs adorn its crown.

The banyan was named after the Indian *banias*, or traders, who sold their wares in its shade. It is also known as the Grandfather Tree, because it is like a patriarch surrounded by endless generations of offspring. Some call it the Many-Footed One because of its numerous trunks. Others call it the Undying Tree. It has lived longer than anyone can remember.

In the center of a small village in India, a many-footed banyan tree flourishes. Every morning at dawn, one of the village women comes to the tree to make offerings. She brings fresh fruit and lays it at the base of a simple shrine. She washes the small stone figures of gods and goddesses and dresses them in clean garments. Then she decorates the shrine with fresh flowers. Using a bundle of twigs as a broom, she sweeps away the dried leaves that have dropped to the ground.

To the people of the village, the banyan is sacred. It is home to their gods. For many generations, they have protected the tree and nourished its spirits with their offerings. In the cool dawn air, the banyan rustles gently. It is a place for worshipping.

As sunlight warms the tree, a pair of egrets arrives with sticks and twigs, which they use to build a shallow platform at the top of the banyan crown. The birds quickly gather leaves and soft grasses to line their nest, for the female will soon lay her eggs. The banyan will hold the eggs snug within its branches. It is a place for nesting.

By the middle of the morning, the space under the banyan is alive with color and sound and movement. Traders from neighboring villages have arrived with many things to sell— chickens and goats, baskets and pottery, fabrics and fruits, spices and flowers. Friends shout greetings and share the latest stories. The banyan shades all the commotion. It is a place for laughing and bartering.

Tooee?
Tooee?

Tuk...
tuk...tuk...

Up in the banyan branches, flocks of noisy birds arrive to eat the ripe red figs. A rose finch calls out sharply as it swoops down on a cluster of fruit. Nearby, a fairy bluebird warbles, and a crimson-breasted barbet sings its steady, hammer-like song. With the arrival of a raucous house crow, a brown speckled koel utters a harsh, staccato cry. The piercing calls echo through the banyan. It is a place for lively conversing.

Kik-kik
kik-kik

In the middle of the day, the sun beats down relentlessly. But under the banyan, it is cool and quiet. People sit in the shade, talking softly. Across the grove, the village primary school is meeting. The children's clear voices sing the day's lesson in unison. The banyan, with its large leaves and broad branches, serves as a huge canopy, sheltering everyone from the dust and heat. It is a place for resting.

In the central trunk of the banyan,
spotted owlets doze through the
heat in a dark hollow. Their bellies
are full of beetles and mice and
lizards caught the previous night.
Their breathing is slow and steady.
The old banyan enfolds the tiny
owlet family. It is a place for
sleeping.

When the school day is finished,
children scamper up the trunks
to perch on the broad banyan
branches. They take turns
swinging on the aerial roots
and sliding down to the ground.
The old tree is filled with the
sounds of their laughter. It is a
place for romping and giggling.

On the other side of the tree,
langur¹monkeys are playing, too.
They chase each other furiously up
and down the long branches, squealing
and chirring excitedly. One swings
through the tree in swift pursuit
of another. The banyan trembles as
the monkeys rush back and forth.
It is a place for wild chasing and
jumping.

As the sun goes down, the old men of the village come to sit under the tree. They discuss the weather, the crops, the state of the world. Sometimes they argue in loud voices. Sometimes they smile and slap one another on the back. An agreement made under the banyan is taken seriously. It is a place for meeting and discussing.

In the evening, the villagers gather
in front of a simple stage set up
under the banyan tree. Far into
the night, costumed dancers act out
ancient stories with graceful hand
movements and intricate footwork.
The audience watches enthralled.
The dark banyan has become a
theater. It is a place for imagining.

Deep in the night, the banyan comes alive again. A colony of large bats, called flying foxes, lands in the branches to feast on the figs. Noisily they chew the ripe fruit, their cheeks bulging out like balloons. As they jostle for position, the bats clamber through the tree, hooking their large thumbclaws onto the branches and shaking the leaves. The banyan quivers with their fanning wings. It is a place for restless rustling.

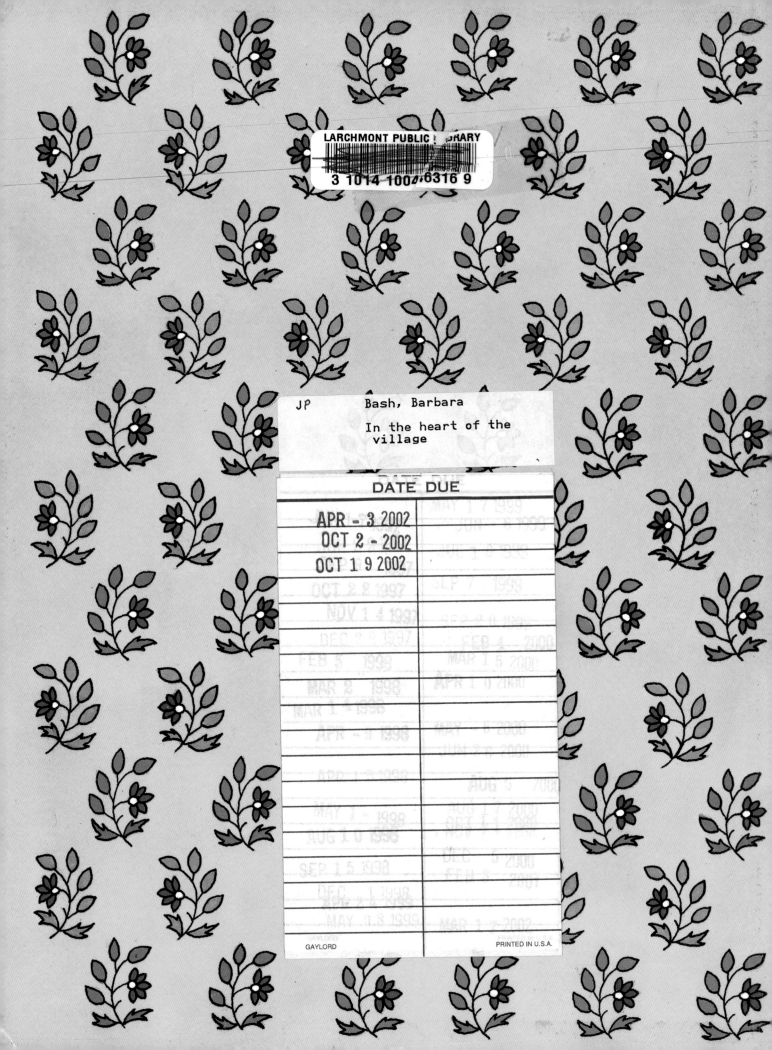

LARCHMONT PUBLIC LIBRARY

3 1014 100 6316 9

JP   Bash, Barbara

          In the heart of the
          village

DATE DUE

APR - 3 2002	MAY 1 7 1999
OCT 2 - 2002	JUN - 8 1999
OCT 1 9 2002	AUG 1 0 1999
OCT 2 2 1997	SEP 7 - 1999
NOV 1 4 1997	SEP 2 9 1999
DEC 2 9 1997	FEB 4 - 2000
FEB 5 1999	MAR 1 5 2000
MAR 2 1998	APR 1 0 2000
MAR 1 4 1998	
APR - 1 1998	MAY 1 6 2000
	JUN 2 0 2000
APR 1 2 1998	AUG 3 2000
MAY 1 - 1999	AUG 1 7 2000
AUG 1 0 1998	NOV 1 4 2000
	DEC 5 2000
SEP 1 5 1998	FEB 8 2001
DEC 1 1998	
MAY 1 8 1999	MAR 1 7 2002

GAYLORD   PRINTED IN U.S.A.